Lynam, Terence

Andy Joins The BMX Bunch

Andy Joins the BMX Bunch

Special thanks to Gregg Ebertowski and Frank Fuchsberger of Wares Cycle Company, Inc., Milwaukee, for their expert advice, patience, and good humor. Thanks, too, to various helpful people at the Milwaukee Public Library.

THE BMX BUNCH
Greg's First Race
Andy Joins the BMX Bunch
The BMX Bunch Turns Detective
The BMX Bunch on Vacation

Library of Congress Cataloging-in-Publication Data
Lynam, Terence.
Andy joins the BMX Bunch.

(The BMX Bunch)
Includes index.
1. Summary: Andy handles disappointment and joy as he tries to earn entry into the BMX Bunch.
[1. Bicycle motocross--Fiction. 2. Bicycles and bicycling--Fiction] I. Mostyn, David, ill.
II. Title. III. Series: Lynam, Terence. BMX Bunch.
PZ7.L979737An 1988 [E] 87-42802
ISBN 1-55532-439-8
ISBN 1-55532-414-2 (lib. bdg.)

North American edition first published in 1988 by
Gareth Stevens, Inc.
7317 West Green Tree Road
Milwaukee, WI 53223, USA

First conceived, edited, designed, and produced in the United Kingdom by Culford Books as *Andy Joins the Gang*, by Terence Lynam, with an original text © 1986 by Culford Books.

Design, this edition: Laurie Shock.
Additional illustrations: Sheri Gibbs.
Series editor: Rhoda Irene Sherwood.
Typeset by Web Tech, Milwaukee.

2 3 4 5 6 7 8 9 93 92 91 90 89 88

Andy Joins the BMX Bunch

Terence Lynam
Illustrated by David Mostyn

Gareth Stevens Publishing
Milwaukee

Andy watched the BMX Bunch sadly. His big brother Greg was a member, but the other kids — Joe, Jennine, and Pete — just laughed when Andy asked to join.

"You're too young," Jennine said. Pete nodded his head in agreement. But they were only a year ahead of Andy in school!

"You haven't even wired bunnyhops. Besides, 10-speeds are strictly zero," Joe said. Greg just looked at the ground.

Every day Andy stood by his old bike, hoping the others would take him along. But he was always left out.

"It's because I haven't got the right bike," he told himself. "I wouldn't be squirrely if my bike looked like a BMX."

Suddenly he knew what to do.

Andy dashed into the house. Minutes later he ran out with a plastic bag, some old socks, a piece of cardboard, a roll of tape, and some felt-tip pens. He'd turn his bike into a BMX!

On the cardboard he colored a big "6." It would be his number plate. He stuffed the plastic bag with socks. It would be his rad pad, attached to the bike with tape.

"I've got the bike. Now I just need the right gear," he muttered, running back inside.

6

6

"I knew I'd be glad I didn't clean my closet," Andy thought. He pulled out an old cap, his winter gloves, and thick wool socks. He pulled his socks over his jeans.

"Gnarly," he thought. "These won't get caught in the gears."

He looked at himself in the mirror and liked what he saw. "Now they won't think I'm a squid," he muttered to himself.

Andy went to the backyard, where his parents were gardening. He began practicing tricks on a ramp made from old planks. Soon he could land neatly on his back wheel. "I've got this wired," he thought. "Soon I'll be doing curb endos better than Joe. Not to mention bunnyhops!"

"Hey, Mom and Dad," Andy asked. "Can I go to the park to find Greg?"

"Sure. But don't be late for lunch," his father answered, with a wave.

"Where'd you get that outfit?" his mother added, smiling.

As Andy rode proudly toward Greg and the others, they pointed at his bike and snickered.

"Definitely not this year's model," Andy heard Pete say in a jeering voice.

Andy cycled off, pretending he had something else to do. He'd fixed up his bike, but that wasn't good enough for the BMX Bunch.

6

Andy shuffled along the edge of the park, pushing his bike. He felt miserable. His bike didn't look so good to him anymore.

Then he heard a noise. It came from the fields below the park. He stopped and listened carefully. It was a voice, calling for help. Squinting into the sun, Andy saw a man, far away, waving his arm.

Andy leaped onto his bike. He raced down a rough, muddy track toward the field. The track was so bumpy that Andy needed all his skill just to stay on his bike.

Going flat out down the hill, Andy spied a stream ahead.

"Uh-oh. I'll have to jump it or I'll bail in the water," he thought. So he charged toward the stream. Near the bank, he pulled into a jump.

"Made it!" he thought. Just then his front wheel skidded on mud. He shot over his handlebars.

Andy rolled to break the fall, picked himself up, and ran to the man lying on the ground.

"It's my leg," the man winced. "I tripped while I was jogging. I think it's broken. You okay?"

"Sure," answered Andy, rubbing his elbow. "I'll get help."

The man looked pale.

Andy flew to his bike and raced up the hill. He didn't even notice that he did a perfect jump over the stream. As he neared the road, he saw a parked police car.

"What luck," he thought. He yelled to the officers, "There's a man in the field. He's hurt his leg."

"Okay, son," the officers answered. "We'll radio for an ambulance. Wait here to show the crew where to go."

POLI

The crew drove up, sirens blaring. Andy led them to the jogger. They carefully lifted him onto the stretcher and then to the ambulance.

Over the hill came the Bunch. They'd heard the siren. Andy felt great. He was in the center of the action! When Jennine and Pete saw what was happening, they turned to Greg and Joe and whispered something. The kids huddled for a minute and then turned to Andy.

"You can join us, Andy, even without a BMX. You can be our mascot," said Joe.

"Ace!" said Andy, thinking mascot was better than nothing. But more good things were in store for him.

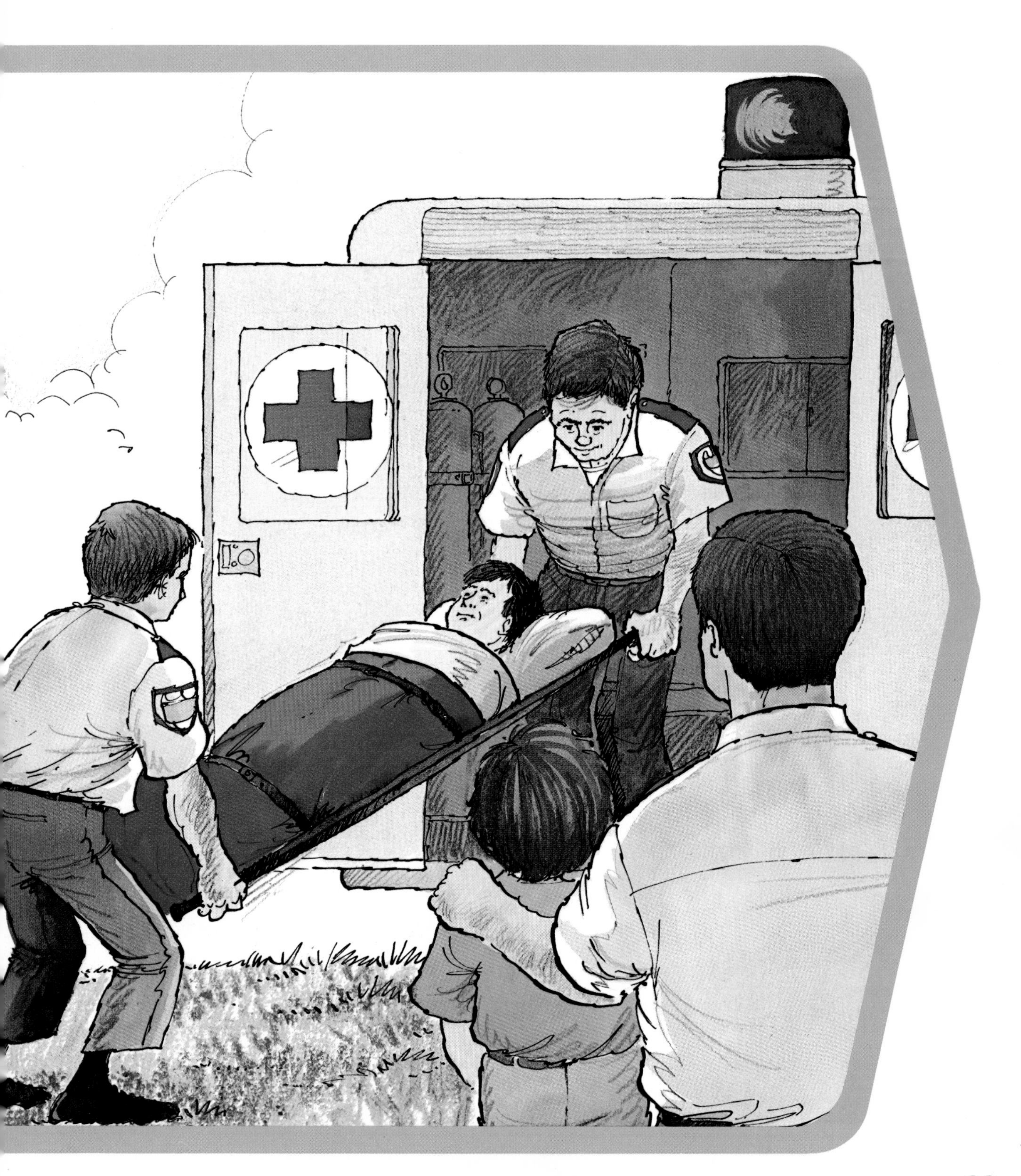

A few weeks later, the jogger came to the house.

"I heard what your friends said to you about not having a BMX. I thought maybe I could do something about that. It's my way of thanking you for helping me." Through the door he wheeled a BMX. It was used, but it was clean. "And in the car is safety gear for you," he added.

Andy beamed from ear to ear. He thought surprises like this happened only in the movies. "It's rad," he said.

"Okay, little brother, you're really in the gang," Greg said with a smile. "Now who can we get for our new mascot?"

BASIC BMX

with chain guard, reflectors, and coaster brakes

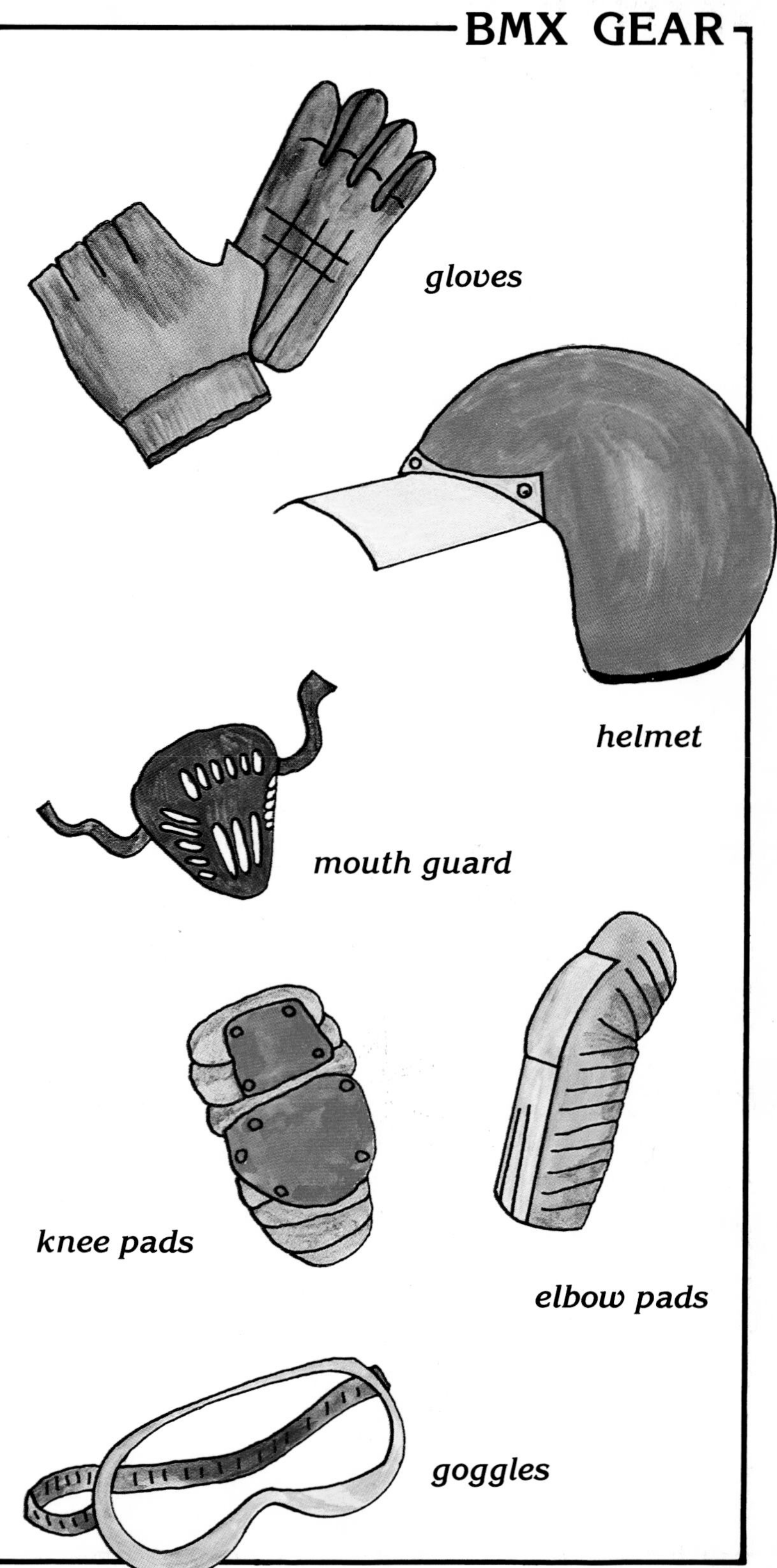
BMX GEAR
gloves
helmet
mouth guard
knee pads
elbow pads
goggles

Safe bikers are rad bikers . . .

Care for Your Bike. Keep your bike in good condition. Check the tires for the right air pressure and for damage done by nails or glass. Tighten loose handlebars, saddle, and spokes. Take your bike to the bike shop to be oiled, greased, and tuned up once a year.

Care for Yourself. When you ride a BMX bike, you should be as careful about yourself and others as you are on any bike. But when you race or do freestyle tricks, you need to be extra careful about protecting yourself from injury. So wear the following protection:

a padded helmet,
a mouthguard to protect your nose and teeth,
goggles to protect your eyes,
a long-sleeved jersey and pants – padded at the knees and elbows (you may be able to buy pads at your bike store),
rubber-soled shoes that will grip the pedals,
sturdy gloves to protect your wrists and hands.

Also have an adult supervise when you practice stunts.

Gnarly rules to know . . .

Follow these basic rules whenever biking in your neighborhood:

1. Obey all traffic signs and other markings on roads.
2. Check with local police about bike rules in your area.
3. Ride single file and on the right side when on the road.
4. Watch for anyone parked on the right who might open a car door.
5. Watch for drain grates, unpaved areas, ruts, and slippery mud.
6. Don't carry passengers or packages that block your view or make it hard for you to handle the bike.
7. Don't ride too close behind trucks or other large vehicles. They will not be able to see you.
8. Wear reflectors at night on your bike and clothing.
9. Be alert at intersections, especially when turning left. Walk your bike in the pedestrian crosswalks at busy intersections.
10. Learn and use these hand signals:

LEFT

RIGHT

STOP

Lots of kids ride bikes these days. The good news is that the percentage of kids being hurt on bikes has dropped since 1940. Good work! You are rad bikers. For information about bicycle safety, write to these addresses:

National Safety Council
Bicycle Department
444 N. Michigan Avenue
Chicago, IL 60611

Bicycle Forum
c/o Bike Centennial
P.O. Box 8308
Missoula, MT 59807

Canadian Cycling Association
333 River Road
Vanier, Ontario
Canada K1L 8H9

BUNNYHOP

Pedal at medium speed toward the obstacle you're jumping.

When at the obstacle, pull bars up and lift front wheel over obstacle.

Push forward and hoist rear wheel over obstacle as you clear with front wheel. Land on both wheels.

CURB ENDO

Pedal at low-to-medium speed.

Keep wheel straight as it hits curb, shift weight forward so rear wheel comes up, and push into bars with stiffened arms.

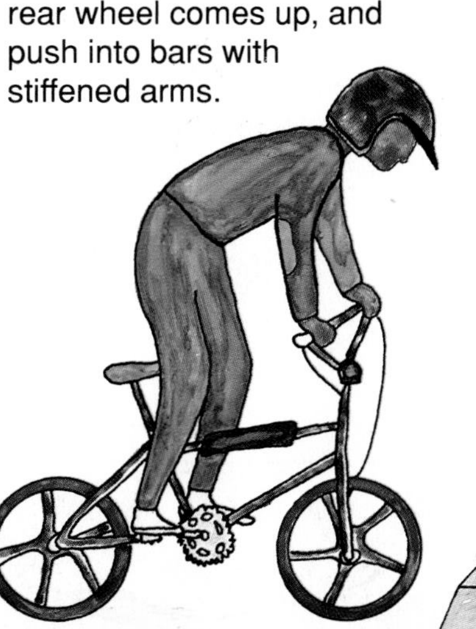

As rear wheel rises, bend knees, shift weight over rear wheel, and keep pushing into bars with stiffened arms so you don't go over the crossbar.

MORE ABOUT BMX . . .

Clubs

BIKE
XING

These clubs hold BMX races and freestyle shows throughout the US and Canada. Write to them if you are interested in their races, prizes, and other awards. BMX racing is so popular, these clubs are moving to get it into the Olympics. Also call your local bike shop to find out about shows and classes in your area for kids interested in freestyling and racing.

National Bicycle League (NBL)
555 Metro Place North, Suite 524
Dublin, OH 43017

American Bicycle Association (ABA)
6501 W. Frye Road
Chandler, AZ 85226

American Freestyle Association (AFA)
P.O. Box 2339
Cyprus, CA 90630

Canadian-American Bicycling Association (CABA)
6520 82nd Avenue, 2nd Floor
Edmonton, Alberta
Canada T6B 0E7

TURNING
VEHICLES
YIELD TO
BIKES

Books

If you'd like to read more about BMX bikes, freestyling, and racing, see if your local library, bookstore, or bike store have the following:

BMX Bikes. Jay (Watts)
Bicycle Motocross Is for Me. Moran (Lerner)
Freestylin' II: The Book. Barrette and Lewman (Wizard). If your bike store has run out, write to: Wizard Publications, 3162 Kashiwa Street, Torrance, CA 90505.

And for more books about the BMX Bunch, read

Greg's First Race
The BMX Bunch Turns Detective
The BMX Bunch on Vacation

Magazines

Check your local library to see if they have these magazines. To subscribe to them, write to the publishers at the addresses listed below:

American BMX-er
...in the States:
American Bicycle Association
P.O. Box 718
Chandler, AZ 85244

American BMX-er
... in Canada:
Canadian-American Bicycling Association
6520 82nd Avenue, 2nd Floor
Edmonton, Alberta
Canada T6B 0E7

BMX Action and *Freestylin'*
Wizard Publications, Inc.
3162 Kashiwa Street
Torrance, CA 90505

Super BMX and Freestyle
Challenge Publications, Inc.
7950 Deering Avenue
Canoga Park, CA 91304

Bicycles Today
National Bicycle League
555 Metro Place North, Suite 524
Dublin, OH 43017

BMX Plus
1760 Kaiser Avenue
Irvine, CA 92714

Also check to see if your local video store has the BMX video called RAD. It's directed by Hal Needham and made by Talia Films II, Ltd.

GLOSSARY OF NEW WORDS — Here are some words you may not know and the pages where you can find them. Some of these words are used by many people; others are used by BMX-ers. After each word is explained, it is used in a sentence.

ace — BMX term: great, impressive, excellent 22
She's an ace freestyler.

bail — BMX term: to fall off the bike 17
He hates to bail in front of his friends.

beam — to smile with a big smile 24
She beams whenever she hears good news.

blare — to blast out loudly and harshly 22
The announcer blared the winner's name.

flat out — very fast 17
The BMX Bunch raced flat out toward home.

gnarly — BMX term: great, excellent 9
She made a gnarly move on the berm.

jeer — to speak in a mocking voice, to tease unpleasantly 10
The audience jeered at the villain.

miserable — sad, unhappy, depressed, awful 13
I feel miserable about the test!

mutter — to talk in a quiet voice, to mumble 6, 9
She muttered to herself after breaking the glass.

pale — unusually light or white 19
Fred looked pale as the lion came nearer.

rad — BMX term: ace, impressive, unusual (from *radical*) 24
He's a rad teacher.

rad pad — BMX term: pads put on bike bars to protect riders 6
My new rad pads make my bike look gnarly!

shuffle — to walk dragging the feet 13
When I'm tired, I shuffle home from school.

snicker — to laugh while trying to cover it up or to hide it 10
They snickered at first, but I showed them.

squid — BMX term: someone who does things badly 9
I hope there aren't many squids at the race Sunday.

squint — to narrow the eyes but not to close them 13
If you must look at the light, please squint.

squirrely — BMX term: shaky, out-of-control biking 5
We all think that was a squirrely move.

wince — to flinch or draw in breath when hurt or frightened 18
My parents wince when they see me do tricks.

wired — BMX term: done well, mastered 4, 9
He had that jump wired right from the start.

zero — bad, boring, nothing (informal) 4
This afternoon has been a real zero.